"HELLO READING"™ books are a perfect introduction to reading. Brief sentences full of word repetition and full color pictures stress visual clues to help a child take the first important steps toward reading. Mastering HELLO READING™ books will build children's reading confidence and give them the enthusiasm to stand on their own in the world of words."

—Bee Cullinan
Past President of the International Reading
Association, Professor in New York University's
Early Childhood and Elementary Education Program

"Readers aren't born, they're made. Desire is planted—planted by parents who work at it."

—Jim Trelease
author of *The Read Aloud Handbook*

"When I was a classroom reading teacher, I recognized the importance of good stories in making children understand that reading is more than just recognizing words. I saw that children who get excited about reading and who have ready access to books make noticeably greater gains in reading comprehension and fluency. The development of the HELLO READING™ series grows out of this experience."

—Harriet Ziefert
M.A.T., New York University School of Education
Author, Language Arts Module,
Scholastic Early Childhood Program

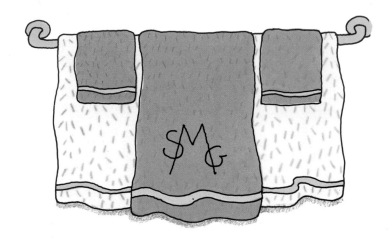

PUFFIN BOOKS
Viking Penguin Inc., 40 West 23rd Street,
New York, New York 10010, U.S.A.
Penguin Books Ltd., Harmondsworth, Middlesex, England
Penguin Books Australia Ltd., Ringwood, Victoria, Australia
Penguin Books Canada Limited, 2801 John St., Markham, Ontario, Canada
Penguin Books (N.Z.) Ltd., 182–190 Wairau Rd., Auckland 10, New Zealand

First published in 1987
Reprinted in 1987

Text copyright © Harriet Ziefert, 1987
Illustrations copyright © Mavis Smith, 1987

Harry Takes a Bath

Harriet Ziefert
Pictures by Mavis Smith

PUFFIN BOOKS

Chapter One
In The Tub

Time for your bath,
Harry Hippo.

Quick, quick,
up the stairs!

Towel...

Soap...

Warm water...

Washcloth...

Everything is ready.
Jump right in!

SPLASH!

Splish splash! Splish splash!

Soap.
Soap up.

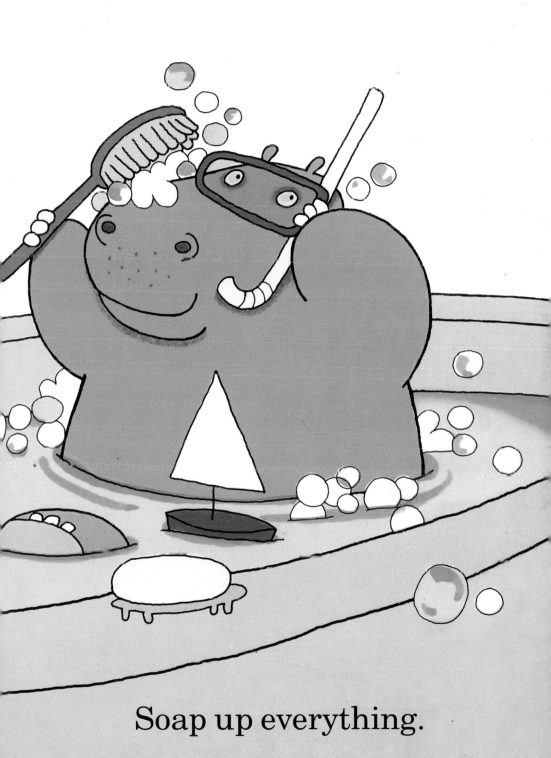

Soap up everything.

Wash.
Wash off.

Wash off the soap.

Clean nose.
Clean ears.

Clean face.
Clean hands.

All clean!

Chapter Two
Out of the Tub

Quick, quick,
out of the tub!

Dry your ears.
Dry your face.

Dry your whole self.
All dry!

Now you can play some more!

The boat sails…

the whale swims...

and Harry Hippo
makes soap pictures
all over the bathroom!

Chapter Three
Clean Up

Clean hippo.
All clean!

Messy bathroom.
All messy!

Scrub the tub.

Scrub the wall.

Dry the whale.

Dry the boat.

Dry the water.

Hang up the washcloth.
Hang up the towel.

Everything is clean.

Good job,
Harry!